THREE
SWORDS
FOR
GRANADA

THREE
SWORDS
FOR
GRANADA

BY Walter Dean Myers

ILLUSTRATED BY John Speirs

HOLIDAY HOUSE / NEW YORK

To Anne Webb
W. D. M.

To Missy, Pyewacket,
and the dreaded Max
J. S.

Library of Congress Cataloging-in-Publication Data
Myers, Walter Dean, 1937–
Three swords for Granada / by Walter Dean Myers;
illustrated by John Speirs.—1st ed.
p. cm.
Summary: In 1420 Spain, three young cat friends join the warrior cats
as they struggle to save their beloved Granada
from the vicious dogs of the Fidorean Guard.
ISBN 0-8234-1676-3
[1. Cats—Fiction. 2. Dogs—Fiction. 3. Friendship—Fiction.
4. Spain—History—Fiction.]
I. Speirs, John, Ill. II. Title
PZ7.M991 Th 2002
[Fic]—dc21   2001059357

Map by Heather Saunders

CHAPTER I

A thin sliver of moon slid through the dark clouds over the city of Málaga. From deep in the night, the soft sounds of a guitar floated above the tiled rooftops. Askia and Paco stayed close to the stone wall as they made their way along the narrow street to Pietro's meeting. The streets were still wet from the rain that had fallen earlier, and Paco walked carefully to avoid the puddles.

"Shhh!" Askia stopped suddenly. He motioned toward a doorway, and the two friends flattened themselves in the shadows. Askia covered the bottom of his face with his cape.

He listened carefully. The two young cats were still, peering into the gloom toward an archway that marked the northern entrance of the town square. Askia's ears perked as he picked up the sound of a low growl. *Dogs!*

"The Fidorean Guards!" he whispered.

"It's late for them to be out of the fort," Paco said. "I wonder what they're up to tonight."

Three huge dogs, their silver gauntlets flashing, swaggered slowly down the street. They were half laughing, half snarling, their attention turned toward a small figure that cowered among them. Askia's eyes narrowed as he recognized the old cat who sold fruits and vegetables in the marketplace. Her eyes were wide, and her gray whiskers pressed against the side of her face. She had raised and sold vegetables for years, but now no cat dared even to come to the marketplace during the day. Nor was any cat free from the terror of the Fidorean Guards.

The Guards, their armor clinking in the night, were pushing the old cat about, laughing as they did so. She

was trying desperately to hold on to the wooden basket she carried.

Askia started to ease his sword out of its leather sheath, but was stopped by Paco.

"Not now," Paco whispered.

Askia knew his friend was right. He had to be patient.

One of the guards snatched a piece of fruit from the basket the old cat was carrying and shoved it into his mouth. The other two laughed and went after the old cat's basket themselves.

The smell of wet dog hair was everywhere. Askia pulled his cape tighter across his face.

The dogs growled and snapped at one another as they ate the fruit in large noisy gulps. Askia saw the old cat slip silently away and breathed a sigh of relief.

"Where is she?" one of the guards yelled.

"Who cares?" was the snarling answer. "We're on duty in the morning. Let's get back to the camp."

The three dogs stumbled and swaggered past the concealed Askia and Paco, the heels of their boots clicking like castanets on the cobblestones.

Askia stepped from the shadows to make sure the dogs had gone on their way. When he was sure, he motioned toward Paco, and they started off again through the arch from which the dogs had come.

The Arch of Tariq led to Via Carola, which itself divided into the high road and the low road. It was down the low road that the two friends made their way.

"Why do you think Pietro called for us?" Paco asked.

"He wants our swords," Askia said. "I'm sure it's for the uprising."

"I didn't even think the elders knew of us," Paco said. "But I guess if you're as brave as we are, the word gets around."

"Too bad he didn't say that we could meet him tomorrow morning," Askia answered. "We would have had time to polish off those three Guards."

"It's time for us to stop passing up the chances to face those filthy dogs!" Paco said. "No matter what happens to us, it will be better than hiding in the shadows, not daring to show our faces in the daytime."

"I saw some kittens the other day," Askia said. "They cover their eyes when the Guards even look at them. Ever since they invaded our city, life has been terrible."

"There are too many of them," Paco said as they neared the sentry who guarded the path to the Sonora, the inn that Pietro used as a meeting place.

"Halt! Who goes there?" the sentry demanded.

"Friends!" Askia answered.

"A friend knows the password," the sentry answered.

"Granada will rise again!" Askia replied boldly.

"Pass, friends." The sentry stepped aside and let them pass.

The windows of the inn were covered with dark cloth to keep the light from showing onto the street.

There was no use in taking a chance that some passing Fidorean Guard would notice the meeting. Once inside, Askia and Paco removed their capes. Other cats were standing about in small groups. Askia recognized some warrior cats from the coast. He saw how tall they stood and how some of them wore their hats down over one eye.

"I was right," he said to Paco, adjusting his own hat. "Pietro is ready to strike back!"

CHAPTER 2

"My friends, we must make a decision." Pietro's voice shook with emotion. "Glaber, the head of the Fidorean Guards, has issued an order that all cats must move across the river to a settlement he has found for us."

"So we can be under his thumb!" a voice called out from the back of the room.

"The only thing that stops them from attacking us is that they can't get us in one spot!" Askia recognized the voice of Tava, who owned a fleet of fishing boats. "We can't make a living cooped up in one small spot."

"Still, we must answer Glaber," Pietro said. "He has given us twenty-four hours to reach a decision."

"And what if we refuse?" One of the warrior cats stepped forward. He was an older cat who had been in many battles, as the missing tip of his left ear clearly showed.

"I asked Glaber that same question," Pietro said. "He simply snarled at me and said that it would be a foolish decision."

"They think we're too afraid to do anything!" Lacy, Askia and Paco's friend, stood up, and Askia saw that she was wearing a sword. "They think that just being a dog settles everything."

"We need to show them we will defend ourselves!" Tava said. "What these dogs want is not just Málaga, but all of our country. Mark my words: next they will attack Granada!"

There were gasps throughout the room. No cat in the room could even imagine the dogs taking their beloved Granada.

"I propose we have a meeting with them," Pietro said. "I will speak to Glaber tomorrow."

"A meeting?" Tava asked. "When did a Fidorean Guard ever respect us enough to have a meeting with us?"

"We are weak and they are strong," Pietro said. "We must at least try to reason with them."

"And if reason does not work?"

"My friends, in these desperate times we must use every weapon we have," Pietro said. He cleared his throat before going on. "You must understand that patience can be a weapon. Know in your hearts that I, Pietro Felini, would rather lay down my life than see even one of us suffer because of these beasts. In my heart I know that we will come through this. Granada will not fall. To this I pledge my sword and my life!"

When the meeting was over, the cats left two by two, slipping out of the door into the murky darkness. The rain had started again. It was cold, and Askia shivered slightly.

"Pietro seemed worried," Paco said when they had gone some distance from the inn.

"He knows how evil the Fidorean Guards can be," Askia said. "And this is just the beginning. But I trust Pietro. He will tell us what to do."

"Suppose, just suppose"—Paco rubbed the end of his nose—"he wants us to fight them?"

"It might come to that, my friend," Askia said. "That's why he invited us to the meeting. Did you see Lacy there?"

"Shh!" Paco froze. Ahead of them a Fidorean Guard leaned against a building.

"What's he doing there?" Askia whispered.

"I don't know. Let's watch," Paco whispered back.

Askia and Paco moved into the shadows. Askia could feel his heart pounding in his chest. It beat even faster when he heard a scritching and scratching along the road. It was the unmistakable sound of a rat. Two shadows in the night. The shadow of the Fidorean Guard filled most of the street. The shadow of the rat crawling near his feet was almost lost in the darkness. From where he stood, Askia could not hear the softly spoken exchange. A moment later the rat scampered off.

"Wouldn't you know they would be friends?" Askia hissed. "Dogs and rats!"

The next morning Askia rose early, washed, and went to look for Paco. He found him with Lacy down at the well in the marketplace square.

Askia, Paco, and Lacy had been friends for years, but it was only recently that Askia had begun to notice how pretty Lacy was. One day he might even get up the nerve to tell her so.

"Lacy's going out to the quarry," Paco said, wide eyed. "She's looking for flint to sharpen her sword."

"Sharpen your what?" Askia looked at Lacy.

"I've practiced fighting with my brothers," Lacy said, her pink nose flaring. "Didn't you see me at the meeting last night?"

"Yes, I did," Askia said. "These small swords of ours

won't be much use against the Guards, but we might as well get them as sharp as we can."

Askia knew that Pietro thought they might have to fight the dogs, but if he was willing to let Lacy come to the meetings, he must have been even more worried than they had thought.

The quarry was almost a mile out of town, and the three friends took their time in getting there. They found flints and sat in the sun sharpening their swords, which were all made from good steel.

"Our swords are much better than the Fidoreans'," Paco said.

"Yes, but they have two swords to every one of ours," Askia said. "And they have armor. Do we really have a chance against them?"

"Are you afraid?" Lacy challenged Askia.

"Afraid?" Askia swallowed hard. "No, of course not."

It was nearly noon when, their swords sharpened, they made their way back toward town. Paco was telling stories about how he had been to the Castillo where the

Guards were camped, and had seen them greedily gobble down their food.

"Then they just slobbered around looking for a warm place to lie," he said. "It was disgusting!"

"What's this?" Lacy stopped and pointed down the road.

Two cats, one limping, the other holding him up, were headed toward them. Askia recognized Tava as the one who was being held up.

"What happened?" Askia asked as they neared the two older cats.

"Pietro was on his way to see Glaber," the badly wounded cat said. "They knew he was coming, and he was attacked on the road by a band of Guards pretending to be bandits. Then they came into the marketplace and thrashed whomever they came across. It looks bad for us!"

CHAPTER 3

All of Málaga was upset. Cats who had lived for years in neatly kept cottages with shaded gardens began to close their shutters and lock their doors. Many who had worked in town now came out only at night.

"How will we live?" Paco asked as he stood in the nearly empty square.

Askia watched as Paco started making his way to where an old tabby had ventured out to sell her meat pies. Suddenly Askia was shoved from behind and a large figure pushed roughly by him.

It was one of the Fidorean Guards.

The dog lumbered across the square, swinging a club at anyone who dared to be in his way.

"Run, Paco!" Askia called over the milling crowd.

Paco turned to see the burly Guard lurching toward him. Without hesitating, he drew the small sword at his side. The Guard stopped in his tracks. His body seemed to swell as he dropped the club he held and pulled his broadsword from its sheath at his side. It gleamed as he raised it high above his head and started toward Paco.

"We'll have to save him!" Lacy's sword was out of its sheath and she was howling as she raced toward Paco's side.

Askia gulped. Even two swords were no match for a full-grown Fidorean Guard, and he saw what Lacy did not see. There was another Guard, the saliva dripping from his mouth, his purple tongue flapping against his dark chin, headed toward Paco from the other side.

Calling on all of his courage, Askia drew his own sword and, hissing to get up his nerve, went flying toward the center of the small square.

The Guard who faced them barked a command, and the one nearest to Paco turned to face Lacy and Askia. The two friends stopped as the huge dog, his lips curled back from his teeth, loomed over them.

The other cats backed off, and in a heartbeat it was only Paco, Lacy, and Askia facing the two Fidorean Guards.

"What do you smell?" one Guard asked, leering and wiping his muzzle with his leather wrist guards.

"Blood!" the other one said, his eyes gleaming in delight.

The two Guards moved slowly toward the three frightened cats, swinging their swords over their heads and then hitting the ground before them so that the sparks flew as sharpened steel hit cobblestone.

"You kill the fat one," the first Guard said, pointing at Paco. "I'll get the other one. Then we can both destroy the one with the long eyelashes. That's one and a half apiece. Enough for supper if they're tender."

"Please . . . please . . ." An old cat, her haunches nearly

bald, lifted her paws to the heavens. "They're so young!"

"And they will never be anything more!" one of the Guards growled.

"Perhaps you should consider the price you will pay for their young lives!" A voice boomed out from the edge of the square.

Askia turned and saw that it was Gamel, the chief warrior of Málaga, who had spoken. One of his soldiers, his wide-brimmed hat down over one eye, stood by his side.

Soon a small group of fighting cats appeared from various spots in the square, each with a sword drawn, each with the hair on the back of his neck puffed and ready for a fight.

"If you filthy dogs have chosen this day to die"—Gamel's voice was low but very clear—"then let us get on with it!"

The two dogs retreated toward the center of the square and stood back to back. Crouching low, they carefully surveyed the crowd of cats around them, letting their eyes stop at each of the warriors. For a long moment, it looked as if a fight to the death would be on.

Then one of the Guards stood up from his crouch and put down his sword. "We will be back," he said. "And when we are, much blood will be shed."

The frightened cats moved away from the dogs as they stomped their way toward the road to the fort they had taken over. The Guards acted as if they had won, but Askia realized that it was they, and not the cats, who had retreated.

"I will remember you, little one!" One of the Guards stopped to point at Askia. He pushed his big head toward Askia's face and sniffed deeply.

Soon, they were gone. Askia took a deep, but nervous breath.

"Aren't you Askia, the son of Damian?" a cat who worked as a scribe in the town library asked, adjusting his glasses.

"Yes," Askia replied hesitantly.

"Well, you'd better head for the hills," the library cat said. "They never forget a scent. And that's the truth!"

"No!" Gamel spoke up sharply. Olivia and Bando, his two fiercest warriors, were by his side. "Askia is young, but he can carry a sword. We all have to be brave. To be less is to be put into slavery, or worse."

"I think you scared those dogs away for good," a storekeeper said.

"No, those curs are always a threat to return," Gamel said. "In the meantime, let's clear out the marketplace and hope that they'll retreat to their holes and be content to lick their wounded pride for a while."

"Go, quickly," Olivia said. "I don't want to have to see anyone lying in the square this afternoon."

The crowd of cats broke up quickly, but Gamel stopped Askia, Paco, and Lacy. From a folded oilcloth that Bando carried he took three swords. They were beautiful swords, made in Toledo with ivory handles. They were heavy, too.

"You three seem to have the courage to face the dogs," Gamel said. "I guess it is time for you to have real weapons."

Gamel gave a sword to each of the three friends. At the edge of the crowd, a Persian whose mate had been killed by the dogs turned away.

"They're just babies!" she cried.

"And remember the pledge of the warrior," Gamel said to the three young cats, ignoring the Persian's pleas. "Our swords and our lives."

Askia felt the weight of his new sword in his hand and took a deep breath. "Our swords and our lives!" he declared.

Paco's house was nearest, and Askia and Lacy watched as he entered and, a moment later, closed the green shutters.

"Were you afraid?" Lacy asked. "When the Guards were coming toward us, swinging their swords?"

"No," Askia said.

He dropped off Lacy at her house and started toward his own. As he walked, his young legs trembled.

"Yes," he said, even though Lacy could no longer hear him. "I was very afraid."

CHAPTER 4

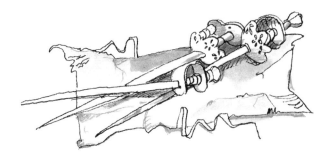

They had carried Pietro to the Sonora. Sophia, his wife, had been called, and it was her wails that Askia heard when he was allowed through a side door with Paco and Lacy. Two cats sat by each window, pretending to eat as they watched the street below. Gamel, his green eyes narrowed to slits, sat by the door. In a corner several cats sat around Pietro, one bathing his wounds as Sophia pulled a shawl about his shoulders. Pietro's lip was swollen from where he had been beaten, and his left ear drooped badly. Askia dropped his eyes when he saw the wise old cat struggle to breathe.

"Never mind my wounds," Pietro said, his voice wavering. "The dogs want to cause as much mischief here as they can. If they can keep our warriors busy with just a few of their soldiers, they will keep us from helping when they attack Granada."

"They will never take Granada!" Gamel drew his sword and held it high in the air.

"Put away your weapon, Gamel," Pietro said. "Don't be betrayed by your own bravery. To fight the dogs now, and on their terms, is to give them a victory."

"These floppy-eared beasts try my patience!" Gamel said. "I don't know how long I can keep my sword by my side."

"You will have your chance soon," Pietro said. "We must be willing to bend so they think we will break."

"I don't understand," Gamel said.

"Trust me," Pietro said. "We will not let the glories of our kingdom go to the dogs. Not as long as there is one breath left in my body."

Gamel instantly knelt on one knee, as did the other warrior cats. They drew their swords and held them high.

"Our swords and our lives!" they pledged as one.

"We must show ourselves with determination," Pietro said. "We must worry them enough to keep a few more of them here in Málaga. Tomorrow we will let the Fidoreans see as many of our warriors as we can muster. We know they will remain loyal to their cause, but loyalty is not enough to defeat us. I will have our warriors march off to the coast just for the day. Give the dogs something to think about."

"We will go with them!" Lacy rushed over to Pietro, fell to one knee, and lifted her sword high above her head.

"No, my young friends," Pietro said. "For you I have still another mission. But first, we must send off our warriors."

Pietro had summoned Askia, Paco, and Lacy to a meeting at a small shop in the center of town. The sun was

bright in the marketplace square. A small covey of doves hunted for seeds along the edge of the grass in front of the white gazebo. Two Fidorean Guards leaned lazily against the stone well, and one slept at the foot of a small olive tree.

"Look there," one of the dogs growled. "You want to have some fun with him?"

The other dog looked over as a lone cat came out of one of the houses.

"There's another one over there," he said, watching as another cat entered the square.

"What's going on?" The first dog looked toward another group of cats coming from behind the gazebo.

Silently, the green and orange shutters facing the square began to open, and female cats, some young, some old, appeared at the windows. Below them the square was filling with cats, many of whom were armed.

"How many of them are there?" the first dog asked.

"I can't tell—they won't hold still," came the gruff reply.

Then, from the windows, the female cats sent up a trembling wail, the wail that thousands of cats had heard for thousands of years before going into battle.

The dogs had drawn their broadswords and watched as the cats formed lines, as though about to do battle. Then, abruptly, all the cats disappeared from the square as quickly and as mysteriously as they had come.

"We need to report this at once!" the first dog said as the wailing subsided and the shutters began to close. "A bunch of stupid cats running around in the middle of the day."

Askia watched as the dogs shuffled off to report what they had seen. When they had gone, the three friends went to the shop where they were to meet Pietro.

"I wonder why Pietro wants to meet us here," Lacy said.

"Now you're asking," Paco said. "You didn't have questions when you ju-jumped into the square and offered your sword."

"I know," Lacy said. "But it's easier being brave when you're caught up in the action. Do you know what I mean?"

"I have a feeling," Askia answered, "that we are not here just to pass the time of day. Pietro is very serious and must want something very serious from us."

"You think it's going to be dangerous?" Paco asked.

"We'll see," Askia said. "We'll see."

The inside of the shop was lit by a set of candles in the shape of quarter moons. The reflections from the candles were caught in a row of dark brass pots hanging along the wall, making them gleam like cats' eyes watching from the burnished gold walls. Pietro motioned for the friends to sit. For a long time he did not speak and they could hear his deep breathing.

"We have made a bargain with Romulus, who claims to know a safe path to the northeast that will lead us to Granada," Pietro said, speaking slowly. "By this route, when the time comes, we will be able to cut precious hours, perhaps even days, off a journey to Granada. If we can secure this route, and if the Guards don't discover it, we might have some small advantage over them."

"You have made a deal with Romulus the Rat?" Askia asked. "He can never be trusted!"

"We don't know that for sure," Pietro said. "That will be your job, to find Romulus and this new route. He and his followers are no more the friends of the Guards than we are. They know that, and I am hoping that the information they give us is accurate."

"But you can't trust a rat," Paco protested. "Rats have never liked us, anyway."

"But they are not stupid," Pietro said. "They know that if we fall, they are next. We are their line of defense against the Guards. I want you three to go to the Plaza el Goremez. There you will meet with Romulus and exchange the money I will give you for the needed information."

"I can't imagine bargaining with Romulus," Lacy said. "He's so . . . slimy!"

"Troubled times make for uncertain friends," Pietro said. "Can I depend on you?"

"You can depend on me," Askia said.

"And on me," Paco said.

"On all of us!" Lacy said. "We won't fail you."

CHAPTER 5

The trip to Far Almadén, the small section of Málaga where the rats made their homes, was not very long. What held them up was Paco, struggling with his new sword, which was almost as long as his short legs. As they made their way through the winding streets, the three young cats were eyed suspiciously by the rats who sold spices and pistachio nuts from wicker baskets.

"Excuse me." Paco spoke to a turbaned rat smoking a pipe in a stall filled with fresh and dried figs. "Do you know where we might find someone by the name of Romulus?"

"Romulus?" The rat removed the pipe from his mouth. "I sell figs, not information. Go away!"

"He didn't have to be so nasty," Paco muttered as they walked deeper into the marketplace.

"Don't look around," Lacy said. "But I think we're being followed!"

"By Guards?" Askia's hand went instinctively to his sword.

"No," Lacy replied. "A rat with a patch over one eye has been trailing us for the last few minutes. I'm sure he's watching us."

"We can split up," Paco said. "And we'll see who he follows—"

"No," Askia said. "We have the silver that Pietro has entrusted us with. The one-eyed rat could be a thief. Let's stay together."

The three friends moved from stall to stall, with Askia and Paco asking if anyone knew of a rat named Romulus, while Lacy glanced back nervously at the rat behind them. When no one said that they knew of him, Askia made for the center of the plaza, where a group of small rats played with an orange ball.

"I didn't think we would have trouble finding him," Askia said. "But if he is here, he will find *us*. We have asked enough questions for him to know that someone is looking for him."

"And if he doesn't?" Paco asked.

"Gracious travelers! Handsome friends!" A high, squeaky voice spoke from behind them. "Are you perhaps looking for someplace to have a nice meal? Ummmm?"

Askia, Paco, and Lacy turned as one to see the rat of whom Lacy had spoken. He was thin, with bald spots all over his stooped body.

"No!" Lacy said quickly.

"What did you have in mind?" Askia asked.

"Well, I have in mind a very quiet place with quite wonderful food," the rat answered. "Yes, quite wonderful food."

"Is it very expensive, this inn?" Askia asked.

"Not for friends of Pietro," the rat answered.

"Then we will follow you there," Askia said.

A constant stream of dirty water ran down the narrow streets of Far Almadén. The patch-eyed rat jumped from side to side to avoid the muck, and Lacy stepped gingerly behind him to avoid dirtying her boots. The place to which they were led was through a heavy wooden door and down a flight of creaky wooden stairs. At the bottom of the stairs were several small tables surrounded by pillows. Two ferocious-looking rats sat at one table. One was greasing his tail.

"Would you like an hors d'oeuvre? Perhaps a bowl of newt-eye fondue?" the patch-eyed rat asked.

"No, thank you," Askia said. "We're here on business. Are you Romulus?"

"Me? Me? Goodness, no," he said, switching the patch to his other eye. "I am but his humble messenger. Be seated. Wait here." He then disappeared into the next room.

"I would hardly call this gracious living!" Lacy said.

"Don't be catty," Askia said. "Just be ready in case it's a trap. These rats are small, but they're crafty."

"I don't think they're that bright," Paco said.

"They found *us*," Askia said. "We didn't find them."

"Here comes the rat who led us here," Lacy said. "And he's brought along a fat friend."

Romulus was the fattest rat Askia had ever seen. He was almost as wide as he was tall.

"I am Romulus," he announced, "chief of all you survey here, master of a thousand trades, musician, poet, and, although I am too modest to mention it, an internationally acclaimed artist."

"We're pleased to meet you," Askia said. "Have you brought the map?"

"But of course." Romulus touched his chest and bowed slightly. Then he pulled a rolled paper from his sleeve and handed it to Askia. "And I trust that you have brought the money?"

"We have the money," Askia said.

"We keep it beneath our swords," Lacy added.

Askia unrolled the map carefully, with Lacy looking over one shoulder and Paco, the other.

"How do we know this route is safe?" Paco asked.

"Because you have the word of Romulus." The rat bowed again. "It is safe; I guarantee it. The Fidorean Guards, a curse be on them, will never discover it, as it passes through a thick grove of garlic. The garlic will erase all scent of those who travel through the grove. And what the dogs—may they always have bad luck—cannot smell, they cannot follow. You say you have brought the money?"

"I don't know . . ." Askia rubbed his chin.

"If you have doubts"—Romulus stood and snatched the map from Askia—"then perhaps you should look elsewhere. Have a good evening."

He turned and started waddling away.

"Wait!" Askia called after him.

"*Yeeeessss?*" Romulus looked back.

"Here is the money," Askia said. He took the purse that Pietro had given him and held it out.

Romulus smiled. "May I offer you a boiled egg? Perhaps I can have my girls dance for you?"

Romulus had gestured upward, and Askia looked to where three veiled rats looked down from a wrought-iron balcony.

"I think we had better return to our part of town," Askia said. He started to ask if the route was the same as the one that Pietro had heard about, but Romulus was already walking away.

CHAPTER 6

Pietro looked over the hand-drawn map that Askia had given him. From the shelves above his desk he took down another map, unfolded it carefully, and compared the two. Tava, who had been in Pietro's study when Askia and his friends arrived, looked at the map also.

"Could be," Pietro said, nodding slowly. "I will have Gamel send some of his warriors to check it out."

"*We* can do it!" Lacy said.

Pietro looked over his glasses at Lacy. "I'm sure you can, my child. But I have something else for you to do." He carefully rolled up the two maps. "We have decided to send the children away. The dogs like to attack children, knowing that it will cause warriors to come to their rescue. If there is a battle, we don't want them in the way."

"We're not children!" Lacy said.

"When you speak like that," Pietro said, taking down yet another map, "you sound like a child. What I want you three to do is to work with Tava."

Tava was a rough cat. He had worked the seas along the coastline for years. He spread out the map that Pietro had taken down and tapped an area with a gnarled and twisted claw. "Do you know this place?" he asked.

Askia looked at it and recognized a lonely stretch of land along the shore. It was too rocky for swimming.

"Hijarah Beach," Askia said. "No one goes there."

"It's a dangerously shallow cove, and there is a wicked undercurrent when the tide comes in too high," Tava said. "Years ago pirates used it to hide their ships. It's a dangerous spot."

"But is it safe from the Fidorean Guards?" Pietro asked.

"I believe so," Tava said. "If we can bring our boats there and board them before we are discovered, we'll be safe. There's not a dog alive who can navigate those waters, and not many cats."

"We can't move the smallest babies," Pietro said, "but we have ten young cats we will send off to the islands, where they will be safe. Can I trust you three to take them?"

"When shall we start?" Askia asked.

"I wish you were already safely on your way," Pietro said. "It must be done quickly, before the dogs know that we are preparing for them. Tava, when can you bring the boats in?"

"Tonight, when the moon is high, and don't be late!"

Tava's throaty rumble sent chills up Askia's spine. "We won't be," he said.

. . .

The ten young cats had been taken to a small church on the outskirts of the city. Their mothers were with them as they huddled in the corners of the large candlelit room. Askia greeted each of the mothers quietly and assured them that the young ones would be safe. There was a last round of kisses and hugs as Askia and Paco checked around the church to make sure everything was clear. Then the mothers went out the front door while Askia, Paco, and Lacy slipped the young cats out of the back entrance to the church.

Lacy warned the youngsters to be absolutely quiet. "So much as a mew or a whimper from any of you and you'll have to deal with me!" she said, trying to look as mean as she could. She looked at one small cat and saw her eyes filled with tears. "And don't worry about your parents. Pietro will see to it that they are safe."

The first part of the journey to Hijarah Beach was through the mountains. Askia was glad because the heavy dogs couldn't chase them as easily up the mountains. The smaller cats were being fairly brave, but Askia knew that they would tire soon.

"Askia!" Paco called out breathlessly.

"What is it, Paco?" Askia stopped and felt for his sword.

"I'm tired," Paco answered, wiping his forehead.

"You can't be tired," Askia said quickly. "We don't have time."

It took the small band nearly three hours to reach a spot where they could smell the salt foam of the ocean. Some of the younger cats were shivering as the wind whirled in gusts around them.

"Paco! You stay here and keep them quiet!" Askia whispered. "Lacy and I will go ahead and see if we spot Tava's boat!"

"Don't ta-take too long," Paco said.

Lacy went to each of the young cats and made sure every one was all right before she and Askia started out.

Above them the sky was dark. Once in a while Askia

could see the half-moon floating behind the heavy clouds. A few drops of rain touched his face. He felt tense and looked over to where Lacy, her ears pointed almost straight forward, moved past some bushes. She, too, sensed danger.

Ahead of them a large dune crested like a huge beast in the night. It was the highest point and they made their way to it slowly, keeping as close to the ground as they could. In the distance the wind howled and whooshed to the rhythm of the lapping waves.

"It'll be hard to see the boat in this darkness," Lacy said softly, bringing her lips almost against Askia's ear.

Askia smiled in the darkness, glad that Lacy couldn't see his face. He was happy she was so near to him. He pushed his head slowly over the top of the dune and looked down at the beach. At first he saw nothing, but then, as his eyes became accustomed to the darkness before him, he could make out the edge of the water. The foamy tide caught what moonlight there was to reveal the crescent shape of the cove.

"Lacy, I see Tava's boat," Askia said. "He's headed toward the shore. We'll be able to make it all right."

Suddenly Lacy grabbed his arm. Askia looked at her and saw her pointing frantically toward the far side of the cove. He narrowed his eyes, then closed them and opened them slowly just as the moonlight, filtering through an opening in the clouds, lit up the beach. Dogs!

"There are at least five of them!" Lacy said.

"We can still pull it off," Askia said. "They're only kids back there, but if they want to, they can move pretty fast. It's dark, and maybe we can get them into the water and onto the boat before the Guards get themselves organized to chase us."

"I think you're right," Lacy answered. "You get the children. They'll need you to talk to them and give them courage. I'll keep an eye on the dogs."

"Okay, but watch me for a signal in case we have to call the whole thing off," Askia said. "Got that?"

"Got it!" Lacy said.

Askia kept low as he made his way back to where Paco and the others were waiting. When he told them that there were dogs at the far end of the cove, they were terrified and one started crying immediately.

"We've got to make the boat," Askia said. "We don't want to go back to Málaga and tell Pietro we have failed. He's counting on us, so let's go!"

With Paco taking the rear and roughly pushing the stragglers, they got to the dune where Askia and Lacy had first spotted the dogs.

"Where's Lacy?" Paco asked.

"I don't know," Askia answered. "Do you see the dogs?"

"No, I don't see—Wait, I see them there!" Paco said.

Askia looked below and saw the dogs. He looked out to sea. Just off the beach, a line of whitecaps was moving quickly sideways. Askia strained to see farther, and there, looming darkly against the vast grayness of the sky, was a boat. Tava had dropped anchor.

"Come on, let's go!"

As Askia pushed the first of his young charges toward the beach, there was a sharp chorus of barking from the spot where he had seen the dogs.

"They've spotted us!" he cried.

"No," Paco said. "Look—they're chasing something."

"Get—get the kids onto the boat!" Askia said.

The race across the beach seemed to be miles instead of the short distance it was. Askia had to half carry, half drag one small cat. Tava was standing in water over his boot tops. He snatched up the first of the small ones and tossed him into the boat.

"There are dogs on the beach!" Askia said to Tava.

"I hear them!" Tava said. "Quick, into the boat."

"I have to go back and help Lacy!" Askia cried.

"She will either escape on her own or be done for!" Tava said. "Get into the boat before we're all doomed!"

CHAPTER 7

"I have to get off the boat!" Askia pleaded, the wind rushing through his whiskers as he looked back toward shore. "Lacy's still back there! I have to go to her!"

"Not possible," Tava called out against the spray of sea air. "You could never swim to shore in this sea and with the tide going out. Once we get out of this cove, I can let you off on a small jetty about two miles up the coast. But even there you'll be taking a chance."

"Then it's a chance I'll have to take," Askia said, pulling his cloak tighter around his neck.

On the deck the young cats huddled together. They

were still frightened, and now they were growing cold. Some cried as they tried to dry themselves.

"We got all the young ones aboard," Paco said, his teeth chattering. "At least they'll be safe."

"*We're* safe," Askia answered, "but what about Lacy?"

Askia felt miserable. He didn't want even to think about what the huge dogs would do to Lacy if they caught her. He squeezed the rope railing of the boat hard as it heaved its way through the water.

"Pietro is thinking about all of us," Tava said, apparently sensing what Askia was thinking. "That's why he wanted to save the young ones. There's no room on this mission for revenge."

Askia knew that if the Guards harmed Lacy, there would be little room in his heart for anything else.

When they reached the jetty, Tava put his arm around Askia's shoulders.

"I think you're being foolish," Tava said. "You're young, hot-blooded, and headed straight for trouble.

And I've got one other thing to say to you. . . ."

"What's that?" Askia asked.

"I wish I had the nerve to go with you."

Askia slipped over the side of the boat and into the cold water. He had taken only a few strokes toward the jetty when he heard a splash behind him. He turned and saw that Paco had followed him. Askia smiled.

It took Askia and Paco the rest of the night to dry out and make their way up the coast toward Málaga. It was daybreak by the time they arrived in a nearby market town. Paco immediately bought a packet of fresh figs and some dried tomatoes.

"I would have preferred cheese and freshly baked bread," he said, popping a tomato into his mouth.

"How can you think about your stomach at a time like this?" Askia asked.

"My stomach is thinking about itself," Paco answered.

"We'll have to be careful. The Fidorean Guards will

surely be looking for us. We can pose as peddlers if you don't eat all of the food."

"Do you think we'll be able to find out about Lacy?" Paco asked.

"The Guards are such braggarts," Askia answered. "They love to hear themselves barking about their accomplishments."

"Their barking scares me," Paco said. "Because I've seen what they can do, even to other dogs."

"How much are your figs?" An old cat in a shawl asked, speaking from one side of her mouth. "Are they sweet?"

"Answer the lady," Askia said.

"Two *pesetas* each," Paco said.

"Two *pesetas*?" One of the old cat's eyebrows lifted and she let out a loud cackle. "They must be made of gold!"

Askia laughed as they went on their way.

It was another two hours before they first saw the western entrance to the city in which they had both been born. The sun was high and the sky was a delicate blue, almost white in its brilliance. Outside the small western gate, a small group of older cats watched as one hit an olive tree with a stick. Askia knew that when the olives had fallen, they would pick them up and have them for their breakfast.

"There is Omar, the letter writer," Askia said. "I'll go to him and ask if he's heard anything. You keep an eye out for dogs who are getting too nosy."

"I'll sell them some figs," Paco said.

Askia went over to Omar and sat in front of him. Omar, as was his custom, did not look up for a long while. When he did, he quickly recognized Askia.

"We were told you were dead!" Omar said.

"It is still my first visit to earth," Askia said. "Who gave you such sad news about me?"

"The Fidorean Guards were around at daybreak saying that two adult cats and a number of young cats were killed on the beach last night," Omar replied, keeping his voice down. "They said it was a warning to those who stood against them. Gamel told us about your mission and so we thought . . . "

"And what of Lacy?" Askia asked.

"Captured," Omar said. "They are going to make her fight in the arena this coming Sunday afternoon!"

"Then she is alive?"

"If the dogs have found a way to make her fight when she is dead, then I will have to give them more credit than I have in the past," Omar said. "What do you know?"

"That the young ones are safely on their way," Askia answered. "And that no cat was killed on the beach last night."

"The news will lift our spirits," Omar said. "And they badly need lifting. They say that Pietro is heartbroken. Tsk, tsk. It is a shame."

"Can you get word to Pietro that we are safe?" Askia asked.

"Yes, of course," Omar answered. "I'll do it myself."

"Who will Lacy have to fight?" Askia asked. "One of the Guards?"

"Wild hyenas," Omar said. "The Guards bring them from Africa for their amusement. They put them in chains and force them to fight. Your friend won't have a chance against them. Whatever did she think she was doing?"

"Only trying to save our world," Askia answered.

Askia was angry when he left Omar, but he knew that his anger would not be enough to save Lacy. Tava had called him young and hot-blooded, but now was the time for him to be more, to reach inside himself and discover who he really was.

As he thought of a way to rescue Lacy, he felt the hair on the back of his neck lift in fear. He took a deep breath and thought of the pledge of the warriors.

"My sword and my life," he said to himself. "For Granada and for Lacy."

CHAPTER 8

The Alcázar sat high on the hill overlooking Málaga. For years it had been controlled by the warrior cats of the city. It had taken months of siege before the Fidorean Guards had overcome the cats, and now it was they who looked down upon the city, and their flag that flew over the stone fortress. During the day the sun reflected brightly off the high walls. By night the shadows were deep and the Alcázar seemed even more forbidding.

"I may not be the smartest feline in the world," Paco whispered as he followed Askia through the bushes that surrounded the fortress. "But I do know that if the dogs catch us sneaking around the Alcázar, we will be made into sausages."

"We have no choice," Askia responded. "We have to find out if Lacy is all right."

"Perhaps you don't have a choice," Paco said. "But I'm n-not in the m-mood to become a sausage."

"They hold the prisoners in cells down there." Askia pointed to a low window. A dim light shone through its bars. Crouching as low as they could, the two cats slid through the underbrush and made their way slowly to the window.

Paco reached the window first, and Askia looked around to make sure that they were not being watched.

"Look!" Paco stiffened. "I can't believe it!"

Askia couldn't believe his eyes. He blinked twice. At a desk in front of the first cell, with his feet up, sat Romulus the Rat! Two other rats sat nearby. Askia recognized one of them as Kip, a gray-and-white rat with a pink, partially crumpled tail.

"We can take them!" Paco spoke softly into Askia's ear. "You take Romulus, and I'll handle the other two."

"No!" Askia took a backward step. "Let's go."

Paco looked dumbfounded. "It was your idea to risk coming up here in the first place, and now we're leaving without even trying to rescue Lacy?"

"Yes," Askia replied. "Let's *go*."

In the cool evening air Askia lowered himself in the high wet grass that bordered the Alcázar. Paco settled next to him.

"What are you looking for?"

"The Guards," Askia said. "We need to know when they make their rounds."

"Oh, great! Let's invite them to dinner!"

For a long time the two cats sat motionless, only their eyes visible through the dense bushes. After a while they heard a clumping sound. Askia sniffed the air.

"Dog breath!" he whispered.

Paco ducked his head down as the Guard walked along the top of the outer wall of the Alcázar, stopped just above where the two friends crouched, and growled menacingly.

Paco pulled his legs tight under him.

Askia opened his mouth so that the sound of his heart beating in the darkness seemed to pound less loudly in his ears. Time seemed to stand still as the dog called to a companion the two cats did not see. Askia felt Paco's back tense and knew that at any moment he would be ready to run. From somewhere came the smell of spiced couscous. Askia hoped it would be calming for Paco.

After a long while they again heard the clumping that was the Guard's footsteps as he continued on his rounds.

"You all right?" Askia asked.

"I w-wasn't afraid," Paco said.

"Do you think you can move now?"

"I tell you I wasn't afraid!" Paco answered.

"Let's go." Askia started down the hill toward the center of town.

"Okay, okay," Paco said, moving closely behind him. "Maybe a little afraid."

Askia and Paco went directly to Pietro's house. They were met there by Pietro's nurse.

"You can't disturb him," she said. "He needs his rest badly."

"I must see him," Askia said.

From the dimness of the inner room came a sound that caught the nurse's attention. It was Pietro, his fur still matted where he had been beaten, his legs unsteady as his frail form filled the doorway.

"Let them in," he said. "When things go badly, we must learn to listen to all voices, however young."

Pietro's room reeked with the scent of incense and burnt garlic. Pietro moved slowly back to his bed and covered his legs.

"What do you have to say to me?" he asked.

"We were at the Alcázar tonight," Askia said.

"The Alcázar?" Pietro raised an eyebrow.

"Yes, sir." Askia remembered that he was still wearing his hat and quickly snatched it off. Paco did the same. "We were surprised to see that Romulus and his slimy horde were guarding the cells. Then we waited outside. There were only two Fidorean Guards."

"We didn't see any other dogs," Paco added.

"And you, Askia, believe that they are very short-handed and that now is the time for us to attack them," Pietro said.

"Why, how did you know that?"

"Well, you must be here to tell me something," Pietro said. "Am I correct?"

"Yes, sir," Askia said, drawing his sword. "There aren't as many of them here as we thought. We can take them!"

"Put away your weapon," Pietro said. "There are no dogs in here for you to skewer. If many of them have already left the Alcázar, they might be on their way to attack Granada. We must try to keep the remaining dogs busy where they are so they can't help the others. It is time for us to act."

CHAPTER 9

A heavy silence hung over the cats gathered at the Sonora. A carrier pigeon had arrived from Granada bearing news that the dogs had indeed attacked, and that the palace was completely surrounded.

"They may have it surrounded," Gamel said, "but they wouldn't dare to attack up those steep hills."

"They will try to starve them out," Pietro said, stroking his silver whiskers. "When they think the cats within the palace have been weakened by hunger and thirst, then they will attack. We have sent messengers to Toledo and Córdoba. In each city there are still Fidorean Guards trying to keep us at bay."

"Pietro, I respect you," Gamel said, standing to his full height. "You were wise in your day, but you are an old cat and your day has passed. We are young and would rather go down fighting than whimpering!"

"Our swords and our lives for our country!" the other warrior cats shouted as they stood.

"Gamel, we have put out the call for cats from every land," Pietro said. "If their hearts are moved, if they come, and if we all fight as one, we might prevail. Even against the might of the Fidorean Guards, we might prevail. Otherwise it will be a catastrophe from which we will never recover. Make sure it is your country, and not your anger, you serve."

"I will do as you say," Gamel said. "For now."

Gamel put his sword back into its scabbard and walked out of the room. Several of his warrior cats went with him. Askia knew that Pietro could not hold them much longer.

"What are we going to do, Askia," Paco asked as they

were leaving the inn, "if Pietro doesn't help us rescue Lacy?"

"Paco, I am going to try to rescue Lacy tonight. It probably won't work and I'll probably be killed by the Fidorean Guards. So if you don't want to help me, I'll understand."

"Askia, I don't want to help you. I want to be home in my bed with a bowl of soup on my night table," Paco said. "But I will be with you, my friend."

CHAPTER 10

The opening Askia and Paco looked for was little more than a hole halfway down the back of the mountain on which the Alcázar sat. Askia remembered first finding the hole when he played there as a youngster. It twisted through the mountain until it came to a narrow corridor among the dungeons beneath.

"Askia, I have to ask this," Paco said. "We found this little opening into the Alcázar, but suppose the dogs have found it, too. What will happen then?"

"Then they will tear us from limb to limb," Askia said. "It'll be terrible. I hope they do me first so I won't have to watch them torture you."

"That's not funny." Paco scrunched his eyes.

"I know," Askia said.

As Askia climbed through the hole, he wondered if the dogs had, as Paco feared, discovered it. He hoped that they would be true to form and far too lazy to do anything about it.

It was a drop from the hole to the ground, and Askia waited, listening for signs that he had been discovered, before jumping onto the damp stone flooring. Paco followed shortly, and they crouched low as they made their way down the corridor toward a dim light. When they reached the place where the corridor curved, Askia, flat on the ground, peered around the corner. At the end of the corridor, a good-luck candle burning beside him, sat another ugly rodent.

Suddenly there was an ear-splitting screech. Askia ducked his head back around the corner and flattened himself against the wall, holding one hand on Paco to keep him from running.

"Will you hyenas shut it up!" the rat squeaked.

"*Oooo-OOOOWWW!*" another hyena howled.

Askia took a deep breath, held it, and peered around the corner again. The rat was stuffing cotton into his ears. He picked up a pebble and threw it at the cage where the hyenas were being held. Then he got up and walked in front of the cage, being sure to stand just out of the reach of the hyenas.

"You boys looking for these?" the rat asked, jangling the keys to the hyenas' cell. He was grinning fiendishly, his beady black eyes glinting in the candlelight. "I thought you guys were laughers. Let me hear you laugh!"

The rat's laughter sounded as if he were choking. He stood in front of the hyenas until he felt satisfied that the caged animals were indeed miserable before going back to his comfortable perch.

"Lacy must be in the other cell," Askia whispered.

"I hope so," Paco said, nodding.

"Well, let's find out, my friend." Askia moved quietly through the darkness.

The rat had closed his eyes, but apparently even with his eyes closed and cotton in his round gray ears, he sensed Askia flying across the floor toward him. Startled, he fell backward, trying to leap from his chair.

By the time the rat had recovered his senses, Askia had grabbed him by his ragged tunic and was holding the point of his sword against the rat's neck.

"Cry out and I will push this sword through your moldy heart!" Askia hissed.

"Don't hurt me! Don't hurt me!" the rat begged. "Did I tell you I've always loved cats? My best friend in school was a tabby. Really!"

"Shut up!" Askia demanded. "Paco, tie him up!"

Paco looked around, found a length of rope, and began tying the rat's paws behind his back. "He stinks!" Paco said, wrinkling his nose.

"Well, yes, I am a rat after all," the rat said.

Askia put the sword to his throat and he shut up.

Askia took the rat's keys.

"Paco, I'm going to see about Lacy," Askia said. "If he moves, cut off his parts."

"Which parts?"

"All of them!"

The four hyenas looked terrible. Filthy and wild eyed, they cowered together in the center of their cell, staring at Askia as he passed.

"Poor wretches!" Askia said to himself, glad not to see Lacy among them.

At first the next cell seemed empty, but then, in a far corner on the floor, Askia spotted a familiar ear barely visible as it came from beneath a thin blanket. It was Lacy. Askia fumbled with the keys until he got the door unlocked and rushed across the cell. Lacy seemed so small, so still. He leaned over her and saw that she was still breathing, but with great difficulty.

"Paco, bring some water, quickly!"

Paco brought the water, and Askia gave it to Lacy, lifting her head gently. Eyes closed, she sipped the water slowly. Then she opened her eyes and saw that it was Askia.

"Oh no, you've been captured!"

"Not yet," Askia said. "Paco and I are here to rescue you."

Lacy sat up and then buried her head against Askia's chest. "I've been so afraid," she said softly. "I didn't want to die alone."

"We have to get you out of here quickly," Askia said. "I don't know how often they change the guards."

"They don't," Lacy said. "It's just that one disgusting rat, with his nasty remarks, who sits out there picking his nose. Between him and the hyenas howling, I thought I would go crazy."

"Is she okay?" Paco asked. "What are you two doing?"

"Nothing!" Lacy said. She was still snuggled against Askia. "Just getting myself together. Did you bring an extra sword?"

"Yes," Askia said, unwrapping the sword he had brought. "Paco, did the rat have any weapons?"

"The rat?" Paco looked back toward where he had tied the rat. "Uh-oh—he's gone!"

CHAPTER 11

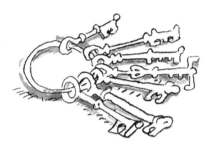

"Let's get out of here!" Askia's eyes grew wide as he lifted Lacy to her feet. "Can you walk?"

"I think I can." Lacy's voice was still weak.

"I'm sorry," Paco said.

"No time for that now," Askia said. "We have to go back down the same corridor we came through before, and we had better not waste time. I'm sure that rat is spreading the alarm right now."

"I'll—I'll lead the way," Paco said as he started out of the cell.

"And we'll be right behind you," Lacy said.

"What's that?" Paco froze in his tracks.

The sound of barking dogs and clanging armor was muffled at first but became clearer as it grew louder.

"We're in big trouble," Paco moaned, "and it's my fault."

"Pietro wanted the dogs to stay in the Alcázar," Askia said. "Well, they seem to be staying."

"At least for as long as it takes to deal with us," Paco said.

"Wait, there might be a way out of this after all." Askia saw the ring of keys still dangling from the door to Lacy's cell. He took them from the lock and handed them to Lacy. "Paco and I will hold off the dogs for as long as we can. You see if you can find the key to the cell that holds the hyenas."

"The hyenas?" Lacy was puzzled at first, then grimaced as she understood what Askia had in mind. "Got you!"

Askia and Paco went down the corridor and stopped at the first turn.

"Good luck, my friend," Paco said.

"No matter what happens, we have done as Pietro asked," Askia said. "The dogs are still here."

The first of the three Fidorean Guards lumbering down the narrow corridor stopped when he saw the tips of two swords pointed at him.

"It's going to be a pleasure cutting you two into small pieces of cat-kabob!" he growled as the other two dogs lined up next to him and drew their swords.

The weapons of the Fidorean Guards were short and heavy. The huge dogs used them almost like axes to pound the swords of their enemies until they broke or until the swords came crashing down onto a hapless victim.

"Now! Get them!" The three dogs advanced toward Askia in a fury, their snouts twisted in hatred, their lips curled, their tongues rolling from the sides of their open mouths.

Clank! Clank! Clank! The sparks flew as steel smashed against steel. Askia and Paco backed up as the blows came, one after another, slowly and deliberately.

The Guards were enjoying their work.

"We'll serve the two of them for lunch," the biggest of the dogs said, stopping for a moment to wipe a string of saliva that dripped from his mouth. "With onions and Spanish olives!"

The trio of dogs roared with laughter and then went back to their deadly work.

Clank! Clank! Clank!

"Askia!" Paco called out in horror as his sword was knocked from his hand and skittered across the stone floor.

"Get against the wall!" Askia called out.

"You go for his head," one dog growled. "I'll cut off his feet!"

Askia stepped back quickly and soon felt his back against the cold wall. With both hands on his sword, he lashed out with every bit of strength in his body. The Fidorean Guard stumbled slightly as he dodged Askia's thrust. There was a moment of confusion as the Guards rearranged themselves to face the two young cats.

"All together!" The biggest of the Guards barked out his order. "Let's finish them once and for all!"

Suddenly a high-pitched scream filled the air. In a flash, four shadowy figures, their red eyes gleaming in the dim light of the tunnel, flung themselves at the dogs. The furious and ferocious fangs of the hyenas were now in the fight, lunging for the throats of the dogs who had tortured them. The sound of bones cracking was matched by the barks and howls of the twisting, turning figures.

Askia felt something pulling on his sleeve. It was Lacy, pulling him away.

Paco had fallen to one knee, and Askia helped him up. Paco scooped up his sword, and the three cats ran as fast as they could through the underground tunnel. Askia found the opening and pushed Lacy into it.

Askia and Paco tumbled after her. Already on their feet, they ran through the brambles until they reached the road before stopping.

"Do you think the hyenas will find this opening?" Lacy was gasping for air.

"I don't know," Askia answered. "And I don't intend to stick around here to find out."

"You go on without me," Paco said. "I'll just hold you back."

Askia looked at Paco and saw that his friend had been cut on his leg. It was a minor wound, but still it needed attention.

"We'll go on together," Lacy said. She tore the sleeve from her blouse and tied it around Paco's leg. A moment later Askia and Lacy, with Paco hobbling between them, were on their way toward the center of town.

"No matter what happens," Lacy said, "at least we're together again."

CHAPTER 12

"Paco, be alert!" Askia spoke sharply as they neared the old marketplace.

There was a deadly silence. Even the well was deserted. A few sparrows sat at the edge of one roof, but they too were quiet. Askia looked around carefully.

"W-what do you think happened?" Paco asked.

"Look there," Lacy said. "There's something coming toward us."

They watched as a wide-bodied cart, half loaded with hay, rumbled toward them. An old cat, his head as white as his whiskers, held the reins of the skin-and-bones horse who pulled it.

Askia stopped the cart and asked the old cat what had happened.

"The Fidorean Guards were suddenly leaving." He wheezed. "A few of them came here and started trouble. They made a big racket when they attacked Pietro's house. He saw through their little scheme, though. He told Gamel to take the warriors and head toward Granada right away, and not to mind him. Gamel took off on the gallop."

"Was Pietro injured again?" Lacy asked.

"He was," the old cat said. "And it looks bad for him. He's at his house now."

Pietro's house smelled of camphor and incense. He was lying on a low cot. A lamp was lit near his head and another near his feet. His wife, Sophia, kneeling by the side of the bed, rubbed his shoulder gently.

"Askia, whatever you did at the Alcázar . . ." Pietro closed his eyes, and Askia could see the pain in his face.

"Whatever you did worked. The Fidorean Guards were even better fighters than I thought. If they had received any help . . ."

"We did our best, sir," Askia said.

"They saved me," Lacy added.

"I know you are tired." Pietro's voice was weak. "But now you must go on to Granada to help with . . . to help with . . ."

"Pietro!" Askia's eyes filled with tears as Pietro tried to catch his breath.

"My time is passed." Pietro looked away.

"You must rest!" Lacy said.

"I close my eyes and I see a free Granada," Pietro said. "I close my eyes and see a Granada rich in glory and in history. I close my eyes. . . . I close my eyes. . . ."

The room grew still. A summer breeze stirred the lace curtains at the windows. The lamp at Pietro's feet flickered and died away.

Gently, Pietro's wife kissed the cat she had loved for so

many years. Then, even more gently, she pulled the sheet over him. Pietro Felini, the elder of Málaga, was dead.

The silence that filled the room grew heavy. Askia looked away from the still figure on the bed, and Lacy covered her eyes.

"I think Pietro would be disappointed that you were grieving for him instead of going to Granada," Sophia said.

"Yes, of course." Askia pulled himself up to his full height. "To Granada!"

"Granada!" Lacy spoke through clenched teeth. "Long may she live!"

CHAPTER 13

"Are you thinking of Pietro?" Lacy asked as the cart they were riding on jostled along the dirt road toward Granada.

"No," Askia answered. "I was just hoping that the weather would be good all the way to Granada."

"There isn't a cloud in the sky," Lacy said. "I think we'll have good weather."

It was true that Askia had not been thinking about Pietro. He had been thinking about fighting against the Fidorean Guards in the tunnels beneath the Alcázar. He could still feel the way his sword trembled in his hands as the Guards' heavy blows crashed down upon him. The dogs had not been afraid at all. There was nothing that he could have done against them, not with their armor and their strength.

Askia didn't want to tell Lacy how afraid he had been, or that he had thought they would surely die. There had been a dreadful moment, as the dogs snarled and came nearer to him, when he had wanted to run. Would he run if he faced dogs again in Granada?

"I am thinking that I am hungry," Paco said. "How long before we reach Granada?"

"Not before tomorrow at noon," Lacy said. "We must keep a sharp eye out for Guards."

"We'll take turns staying awake," Askia said. "I'll take the first turn. Paco, there is a half loaf and some cheese in my bag. Take it."

Paco took the bread and cheese and snuggled into a corner. Lacy, who had taken off her boots, closed her eyes and purred contentedly as the last rays of the sun warmed her face.

Askia wondered if she was afraid. She seemed fearless.

"I am not afraid!" Askia told himself.

"What was that?" Lacy asked.

"Nothing," Askia said. "Get some sleep."

Askia closed his eyes for a moment. *Whatever happens, will happen.*

He stayed awake even when it was Paco's turn to be on guard, letting his friend rest against the side of the cart. Just off the road were the campfires of the gypsy cats, and the soft sound of their music, a slow wailing punctuated with the staccato clickety-clack of castanets, was a reassuring sound in the night.

Lacy had awakened and taken over for Askia. He had fallen into a deep sleep, dreaming of fishermen stretching their nets along Málaga's sunny beaches, when he felt himself being shaken.

"What is it?" he asked.

"The wagons up ahead are being stopped!" Lacy said, her voice sharpened by the tension of the moment.

Askia nudged Paco awake with his foot as he drew his sword. He peered up ahead into the gentle mist of early morning. What he saw clearly was that it was armed cats, not Fidorean Guards, stopping the wagons. They had reached the foothills of Granada.

"The dogs have formed their ranks to the north of the city," a sleek, amber-eyed cat wearing the jaunty hat of a cavalier said. "We are forming our lines to the west. Go there and you'll be welcomed by our forces."

As the rising sun burned off the early mist, Askia could see, high on the hill overlooking the city, the Alhambra, the palace of the Moors and the sacred home of the cats. It was a magnificent sight, and he could feel, if not his courage, at least his determination, returning.

"Askia, I'm afraid," Lacy said.

"What we do, we do for all the cats in the world," Askia replied. "And for Granada!"

"Look over there." Paco pointed to what looked like a thousand flags waving in the wind. "What is that?"

Askia looked. What he saw took his breath away. Arrayed before him, all across the plains below the great Alhambra, were row after row of cats. More cats than he had ever seen, had even imagined, in his life. Their uniforms brilliant, their flags flying in the warm summer breeze, they were magnificent.

"There are cats from everywhere!" Lacy said.

And she was right. Askia saw French cats, their berets tilted at an angle over one eye. There were English cats with longbows and Spanish cats from Cataluña. There were Italian cats from Catania and dark Asian cats from Katmandu. There were male cats and female cats, all warriors, and most of them just a little older than Askia, Lacy, and Paco.

"Where are you from?" a tall cat wearing leather boots and carrying a musket asked.

"Málaga," Askia answered.

"The company from Málaga is forming over there, at the foot of that olive grove," the cat said.

The olive trees, their leaves tinged with silver, glistened in the bright sunlight. At the foot of the tree, beneath the flag of the city of Málaga, Askia recognized Gamel sitting on a spirited white horse.

"We can't let them back us up," Gamel was saying.

"Parry their blows with the hilts of your swords. Don't let them use their strength directly against your blades."

Askia took a deep breath and let it out slowly. He was so afraid that he could hardly think straight, but he knew he would not run away.

It was late in the afternoon when Gamel was given the order to have his warriors prepare for battle. The Fidorean Guards had completely surrounded the Alhambra, gathering around the steep hill upon which it sat. The army of cats had, in turn, surrounded the Guards, and the dogs had now turned to face them. Gamel had all of his company form lines and went down each line to inspect them. When he got to Askia, he looked into his eyes.

"I am glad to see you here," he said.

"Pietro is—"

"I've heard," Gamel said. "But he was right about you, and he was right that we will not let Granada fall."

Gamel kissed Askia on both cheeks and moved on to Lacy, and then to Paco.

"Warriors, we are facing a determined foe," Gamel called out. "But we have the bravest hearts in all the world. Remember what it is we pledge today. Our swords and our lives!"

Askia could feel his heart pounding as he marched with the others to the field of battle. When Gamel stopped them, Askia could see thousands of cats on either side of him.

But across the field were the Fidorean Guards. There were so many of them, Askia thought, and their swords, held high to catch the light, made his knees weak.

There was the sound of a trumpet on the wind, and slowly the dogs began to move forward. They formed a huge square, their shields before them, one against the other.

"Archers, aim low!"

A row of female archer cats stepped forward, drew their bows, and knelt, ready to fire their arrows.

"Catapults ready!" Gamel shouted.

"Archers, hold!"

"Catapults . . . now!"

Askia watched as the catapults sent hundreds of stones into the air.

The Fidorean Guards saw the stones, too. They stopped, moved even closer together, and then, as one, brought their shields over their heads as the stones started their downward arc.

"Archers! Away!"

The archers let loose their arrows, aiming low as they had been instructed. Now the dogs were confused. Some held their shields high to protect themselves from the stones shot from the catapults. Others lowered their swords to stop the arrows. The solid formation the guard had formed was broken, but now, with their bloodcurdling cry of "HAVOOOOC!" they charged across the field toward the waiting cats.

"Courage!" Gamel called. "Courage!"

Askia felt his legs shaking as the dogs drew nearer and nearer. Then, roaring and barking as they closed in, the dogs attacked! Askia lifted his weapon just in time to avoid being cut in two by a wildly swung sword. The force of the blow

sent him backward. He could feel his sword vibrating, and it was all he could do to hold on to it. Another huge swing and he nearly went down. Gamel's words came back to him. Parry the blows—don't block them!

Another blow came crashing down at Askia. This time he moved the hilt of his sword just enough to deflect the sword. It came very close. He felt himself edging backward with each blow.

"Your sword has a point, my friend!" an older cat called to him. "Use it!"

The dog who came at Askia had a big head and wild eyes. He swung blow after blow, and it was all that Askia could do not to close his eyes. He parried one blow and then another. From somewhere he got up the nerve to thrust his sword at his enemy. It struck, not deeply, but Askia had felt the hit. The dog growled and crouched low. He moved forward again and swung his sword like an ax. Askia parried just in time and felt the sword cut through his whiskers. Askia reached out with his sword again, pointing it straight at the hairy chest before him.

The dog stopped for a moment to look down at his chest and was immediately struck by another sword in his side. Askia glanced over. It was Lacy!

The dog moved back and brought his shield in front of his snout. They were all moving back! At first they moved slowly, swinging their swords at anything within reach, and then faster. Soon they were running, their tails between their legs, scampering back to their camp.

Gamel stopped his warriors and told them to regroup.

Askia looked around him. There were cats lying on the ground, wounded. Some were just sitting, trying to catch their breaths. Others knelt in silent prayer. They had held off the attack of the Fidorean Guards!

All over Granada it was the same. The cats held! The Fidorean Guards retreated. By nightfall the dogs had formed a line and were limping back to their own country.

Askia searched for Lacy and Paco, and found them both. He hugged and kissed them.

"I'm so glad you're all right," he said.

"I'm so glad I'm all right, too," Paco said.

The army of brave and dedicated cats spent the next two weeks in Granada, making sure that the Fidorean Guards did not return. Then Gamel led the cats from Málaga back to their homes.

Celebrations were held all over the city. The soft sounds of flutes and guitars replaced the terrible clatter of clanging swords. Once again the busy marketplace was full of smiles during the hot, balmy days. Once again the cool evenings found the citizens of Málaga strolling along the waterfront.

It was on such a night that the three friends came together again to watch the boat bring back the kittens they had saved.

"Look how they play with one another," Askia said. "Yet one day they will grow and be brave enough to defend their country and their families."

"Like you?" Lacy asked.

"I'm not that brave," Askia said. "I don't think I'll ever be as brave as Gamel."

"You're brave enough for me," Lacy said. "And brave enough to save Granada."

"I was never so scared in my entire life," Paco said. "I'm still a little shaky."

"But the Fidorean Guards are gone, and we're free to live our lives in peace," Lacy said. "That's the most important thing."

"And free to be best friends forever," Askia said. "And somehow that means so much more now."

The three friends sat together and watched the moonlight glittering on the gently rolling sea. Askia knew that this was the moment, and the friendship, they all deserved.